THE BLACK STALLION'S GHOST

BY WALTER FARLEY

RANDOM HOUSE 🏠 NEW YORK

*For our Pam,
who brought Joy and Love
to all those she touched and
who truly lived every day of her life.*

Contents

THE GHOST

1

The man was almost invisible against the backdrop of the dark velvet curtain. His tall figure was clothed completely in black and his hair and skin were black as well. He raised a large and corded hand, one capable of great strength, to touch the silver-gray body of the mare beside him. His hand was so light upon her that he might have been touching a ghost.

She responded to his touch by a slight fluttering of her ears. It was enough for him to know that she was expectant and ready to enter the ring. He parted the stage curtain a bit in order to see the spacious hall and audience on the other side.

It was his first visit to Stockholm, Sweden, and he was impressed. The hall was more like a theater than quarters for a circus. Festively illuminated, it was a pleasing sight on that bitter-cold winter night. Red plush seats in ringside boxes and rear and side balconies rose to what seemed an incredible height. Every place was taken and all eyes were on the single ring where Davisio Castini and his bareback riding troupe were bringing their act to its finale.

The orchestra played a stirring march while the heavy horses thumped about the ring. The type did not appeal to him but he knew they had a place in the circus. He cared less for the feathered head plumes and jewel-studded breast collars they wore.

He touched his mare again and her ears pricked forward, awaiting his spoken command. There never would be any glittering ornaments on her, he promised himself. No plumes. No jewel-studded bridles. No colorful ribbons woven into her mane or tail. Nothing, not even a halter. By her movements alone she would overwhelm the audience.

He pressed closer against the curtain to avoid being seen. No emotion showed on his face; never had he allowed it to betray his feelings, in or out of the ring. Cold and masklike, and with deep-set unblinking black eyes, it resembled a piece of classic sculpture. Always he had sensed people's fear of him and, while he found it amusing, never attempted to change it.

The bareback act came to an end and there was a fanfare of drums from the orchestra, followed by a polite wave of applause from the large crowd. He listened and decided that, despite the air of festivity, the audience was as cold as the night outside.

Nervously, now that it was almost time for his mare to enter the ring, he removed a small gold figurine from his pocket and rubbed it gently. The growing warmth of the statuette in his large black hands gave him courage and confidence. He believed strongly in the powers of the small figurine, for his Haitian blood and heritage had made him more superstitious than most men.

The ringmaster, wearing frock coat and top hat, signaled him to be ready. *"Bientôt, ma cherie,"* he said quietly to his mare.

The fanfare of the trumpets cut the air once more. Then the shrill notes ended and the voice of the ringmaster rang through the spacious hall, as clear and commanding as the silver trumpets had been.

"Ladies and gentlemen and children," the ringmaster announced in Swedish, *"the Circus Heyer takes great pleasure in presenting The Ghost. . . ."*

As the horseman listened to the introduction, he thought of the great number of languages in which he had heard it given. For more than ten years he had traveled with different circuses throughout Europe, as far east as Siberia as well as to all the British Isles.

He knew little Swedish, but it made no difference, since the introduction was always the same. Like the music which would follow, he had composed it himself, so he and his mare always felt at home in whatever country they played.

There was a long pause as the lights in the great hall dimmed until the audience sat in almost complete darkness. This, too, he insisted upon wherever he played—ten seconds, at the very minimum, to silence the spectators and prepare them for the ethereal beauty of what was to come.

He slipped the thin leather halter off the mare's head, acutely aware of her readiness to obey every cue.

He had no doubt that she looked forward to the gala stage on the other side of the curtain and the elegant audience that would be watching her.

The ringmaster had moved to the orchestra pit, leaving the ring in total darkness. *"The Ghost,"* his introduction continued, *"a god-horse, one no longer earthbound but of dancing fire, a winged Pegasus . . ."*

The man holding the mare would have preferred it if the introduction had ended there. He wanted nothing more except complete silence and the darkness, followed by the first haunting notes of the music. However, the owner of the Circus Heyer, like most of the others he had worked for, insisted that his name be mentioned, since it was familiar to circus audiences throughout the world. He had given up arguing that it was only the mare's performance that mattered.

". . . A supreme exhibition of horse training directed by the world's first horseman in the art of dressage and haute école, *Captain Philippe de Pluminel, formerly with the Cadre Noir of the French Cavalry School!"*

"Entrez," the captain whispered softly to the mare. She went forward while he remained behind the curtain, his face showing no trace of nervousness or even excitement. He was a man in full command of himself and the horse in the ring.

Into the complete darkness and the silence came the first sounds of the music. It was faint, almost impossible to hear, and then it swelled, flowing throughout the hall. The captain could sense the rise in tension as the people waited for something to happen. They were under the spell of darkness and expectation.

He knew that few among them realized that his

music had been composed to create just that feeling—
that *anything* might happen. It faded away again to the
faintest of sounds and, finally, stopped as abruptly as it
had begun.

The captain smiled in the darkness. The audience
was still silent, but he knew that they were growing ap-
prehensive. They must be straining their eyes and ears
for the faintest sound or movement from the ring.

Once again the music came, this time with a
dreamlike slowness, as if carried on a summer wind,
and barely audible. It echoed through the hall, percus-
sive but muted with a thin, haunting piping sound.
Then the rhythm became brisk, followed by a long
flute passage, a new movement, as gentle as rain, the
soft sounds stealing through the hall, mysterious, re-
mote and ever-haunting.

Suddenly the spotlight came on to bathe the mare
standing quietly, peacefully, in the center of the ring.
Her head was lowered, as if she were grazing in pasture
rather than standing in the tanbark of a circus ring. She
would remain that way until her next musical cue—a
shrill piping note, constantly repeated.

The captain's eyes never left her silver-gray body.
A moment went by while the mare remained ghostly
still, as if under the deep spell of the music. The sounds
carried far, the notes seeming to stretch out infinitely. It
was weird, uncanny music, to him who had created it
as well as to the audience. He listened to the receding
echoes and could almost hear the cries of distant birds.
It was ominous music and yet with it came a sort of joy,
an excitement, an intoxicating sense of danger.

He heard the first of the piping notes faintly in the

background. It was the signal for his mare to begin. He watched her lift her small head and gaze into the darkness outside the ring. She seemed startled. Her tension mounted as the notes were repeated and became louder.

She turned her head as if she didn't know where the sounds were coming from, or why. She began trotting around the ring, slowly at first, but as the notes quickened so did her flying feet. The notes became a horrible whistling. She slowed abruptly, as if realizing there was no running away from the crackling noise. The notes became slow with her strides, even sly, with long pauses in between.

She continued trotting around the ring but now her strides kept time with the notes. She paused with each syncopated step, dancing as she moved in measured, cadenced strides, the embodiment of supreme grace and beauty.

The captain missed nothing as he watched her floating about the ring with no movement of ears or nostrils. *Like a ghost,* he thought, *her namesake—but a ghost only in her lightness of foot.* She was very much alive, his mare. Everything in her was attuned to the music. She raised her legs high in time to the rhythm.

The pauses between the shrill notes became longer. Obediently, she slowed her strides without lessening their lofty height, giving the impression of barely touching the ground as she moved forward.

He watched her perform the *passage,* and wondered how anyone in the audience could not be captivated by her dancing fire, even if ignorant of the noble art of dressage in its highest form. There was no evidence of her great strength being tried in the disciplined, controlled trot. Instead, it was as if she performed that slow, measured pace for her own delight.

Did the Swedes appreciate what she was doing riderless? he wondered. *Without benefit of physical commands of hands and legs to prompt and guide her into the movements of* haute école? Almost every circus could boast of having a horse and rider skilled in dressage. But no horse, so far as he knew, could give such an exhibition alone! It had taken years of hard work to achieve this perfection!

The music grew louder, flowing around him and into the hall. The piping notes in the background were barely audible but he heard them, as she did. They became more distinct, more commanding, and her movements changed quickly.

She slowed her forward movement still more without the slightest change in gait or lofty carriage. Suddenly she was trotting in place, her hoofs faultless in their timing, and dancing like the "god-horse" the ringmaster had announced. Truly, she did not look earthbound!

The captain watched her perform the *piaffe* with critical eyes, and saw no mistakes. In all the years they had worked together, she had never been as faultless as now.

Finally the music stopped and she was released from the *piaffe*. She made a slow circuit of the ring, then stopped to stand magnificently in the spotlight as if awaiting the acclaim she knew she deserved.

With great effort, the captain controlled his anger at the crowd's polite but restrained applause. In every other country they had played she had received a tumultuous ovation at this moment. His disappointment was not for himself but for her. He knew she missed the cheering. Always, she reacted to a stirring wave of applause by working better.

As if in a great cathedral, the crowd waited without word or sound for the mare to go into her next display. The captain resented the coldness of the elegantly dressed audience. Were the Swedes unimaginative as well as dull and unappreciative? Were their reactions based on what they knew was expected of them as a nation of reserved and practical people?

He was angry inside and he sought to quell the mounting hot temperament of his own blood. Yet a freezing coldness was there, too, controlled but with an ever-creeping deadliness. He concealed it well. Nothing showed in his face. He looked calm and dispassionate, his eyes a steady, black stare.

He watched his mare as she quickly responded to the clash of cymbals by breaking into a canter. The cadence of her hoofs picked up as if she had been eagerly awaiting the change of pace. And yet her quickening strides were more floating than driving, so she appeared no more earthbound than she had at a trot.

Faster and faster she circled the ring until she was in a gallop. Suddenly she spun on her hind legs, pirouetting in place and spinning in a small circle as if she sought to drive a hole into the tanbark with her hoofs.

The music rose in a great crescendo and a moment later she lifted her forelegs in the air at an acute angle while balancing herself on her hind legs. She held this pose for several seconds before coming down.

The captain waited for the crowd to applaud her

levade, and when the rippling of applause finally came, he smiled. She was reaching them and she had much more to give.

To the roll of the drums, she rose again in the *levade* and finished with four jumps on her hind legs that carried her across the ring in the *courbette*. Only then did she bring down her forelegs and trot slowly around the ring, still swaying to the music, forever dancing.

His heart went out to her, for he knew how much she enjoyed her dancing. It was the woman in her, he thought. No stallion, no gelding he had ever trained could equal her lightness of foot, her natural rhythm.

He no longer cared if the crowd applauded or not. It made little difference now. He was celebrating with her these difficult movements brought to perfection by their many years of work together. Her own will had merged with his. She was indeed one with him in all respects.

Now, nearing the end of her performance, she was in the center of the ring. The music faded and only the shrill notes of the flute were heard. They became louder, as they had been at the beginning, and she responded quickly to these signals. Everything in her was alerted. It was evident in the movement of her muscles beneath the spotlight, in the quivering of her nostrils and the ceaseless twitching of her ears.

Once more the notes were so constant that they became a horrible whistle. As they approached their highest pitch, it appeared that she could no longer tolerate them and sought escape. She sprang into the air with her forelegs stretched out while drawing her hind legs beneath her in the difficult *ballotade.*

The captain was unmindful of the applause. He heard only the horrible whistling notes and his eyes were only for the mare. Again she rose from the ground. This time in midair she kicked out her hind legs savagely in unison with her forelegs as if to ward off a pursuer. Truly, she appeared to be a winged horse, a Pegasus, soaring through the air, her head raised high and her mane and tail flying!

The breathtaking *capriole* was the climax of her performance, and when she had finished the lights in the great hall went on, growing in brightness and brilliance. The mare stood still in the center of the ring, her ears alert, her nostrils flaring.

The ringmaster motioned the captain forward and he joined his mare reluctantly, standing beside her in his dark evening clothes.

He raised his hand to acknowledge the ever-mounting applause of the crowd when they saw him. Like her, his movements were proud, cool and controlled. It was not as he wanted it. They applauded now because he stood with her beneath glaring lights and they were able to see and judge the act for what it had been—a serious exhibition of horse training.

Few Swedes cared about imagination of any sort, he decided. They wanted their Art to be obedient and useful, nothing that might ever excel and surpass life itself. They had seen no ghost-horse, no winged Pegasus—only a well-trained animal. They would not waste their time pursuing idle fantasies. They had no part in his own imaginative world.

He had little use for such practical people, and he did not want to be influenced or changed by them and others of their kind. He ceased listening to the applause and concentrated only on his mare and his own thoughts. He stroked her neck beneath the gray mane.

This was to be his last circus performance in Europe, for he had agreed to a contract with Ringling Bros. Barnum and Bailey in the United States. It meant a well-deserved vacation for him and his mare; they would not have to work again until he joined the Ringling Circus at its training quarters in Florida.

He would leave this land of coldness behind to pursue something he'd wanted to do all his life. He would visit Haiti on his way to the United States and find out for himself what the land of his ancestors was truly like. He had heard many strange things about Haiti and a legend that was filled with impossible events—one he'd been told by his father, when a child, passed on from generation to generation as part of their heritage. He had an overpowering urge to learn more about the legend, and because he believed in signs and omens, the contract with Ringling Bros. coming at this time pointed the way.

The applause continued and he saw some children standing up and hanging over a balcony rail, waving their programs at him. He waved back, knowing they had seen The Ghost as he had planned they should see her. The circus was for children and the imagination of children.

The lights dimmed except for the yellow spotlight as he backed his beloved mare out of the ring. Little did she know what he had in store for her across the ocean. He wanted her to have a foal and he had found the stallion that was right for her in every way. He had seen him on Swedish television only that week, a horse called the Black, the American champion, winning a great race in Florida. That he should find such a stallion now, after so many years of searching, was still another sign that pointed the way for him. He was determined that nothing would keep him from acquiring the Black for his mare. He was a man who took what he wanted. He was as remorseless as he was powerful.

The applause continued long after he stepped behind the black velvet curtain, but he did not return to acknowledge it.

THE BLACK STALLION

2

The stallion tossed his head, sniffing the spring air with dilated nostrils. He was a coal-black silhouette against the golden light of early morning. Within his great body was a fierce, insistent, almost intolerable longing for a mate. He became more excited than ever when the wind brought the sharp odor of mares to him from a distant pasture.

He gave a sudden shrill neigh which was clearly meant for the mares he could not see but knew were there. He gathered himself, rocked back on his hindquarters, and plunged forward. The morning echoed to the wild pounding of his hoofs as he raced down the field, his black mane and long, thick tail gleaming brilliantly in the sun.

He kept close to the arrow-straight fence which separated him from other paddocks and fields like his own, all green with lush grass. When he came to the end he stretched his head high, peering over the top board.

Now he could see the mares and he shrilled again the high, clear note of the stallion—challenging and passionate and urgent with life. His calls shattered the morning stillness and some of the mares raised their heads and turned his way. A few began to gallop in wide circles but the majority continued grazing as if they had not heard his love call. He repeated his clear, happy neigh of desire, hoping to attract the running mares—but soon they, too, turned away from him and continued grazing.

In ever-mounting fury and frustration he raced back and forth along the high fence, displaying all his speed and strength and fire. When he stopped it was only to paw the ground and send clods of earth flying. His neigh changed with his stomping; it became more metallic and threatening, more demanding than loving.

The mares raised their heads again and listened. They saw the stallion in all his maturity and masterfulness. They listened to his calls, which rang so defiantly across the field. Then, as one, they took flight, streaming away from him in a tangle of bodies and plunging hoofs.

He watched them go, his eyes sparkling with a savage fire. He continued snorting and the veins beneath his silken coat swelled. He rushed madly in a wild gallop that sent the earth flying from his hoofs.

Later, when his anger was spent, he sought the shade of a towering oak tree. There he carefully lowered his body to the ground. He rolled over, his legs hanging limply in the air, and rubbed his back and hindquarters against the cool turf.

Alec Ramsay had watched his horse from a

perch on the top board of the fence. "Is that the way to behave?" he called to the Black. "You should know better."

The stallion continued rolling, paying no attention to him. It didn't matter; Alec had learned long ago to speak to the Black whether or not the stallion listened.

Alec smelled the pungent odor of steaming cane juice in the air and looked beyond the green carpet of fenced pastures to the tall chimneys of a distant sugar mill. Long columns of gray smoke floated and wavered above the stacks, scenting the land with an almost over-powering sweetness. Sugarfoot Ranch was an appropriate name for this place, he decided.

After having spent the previous two months in the teeming coastal city of Miami, Alec had not expected south-central Florida to be as enjoyable as it was. Most winter visitors, like himself, were lured to the coastal areas and never saw the vast, sparsely populated region on the edge of the Everglades.

He turned his face to the tropical sun, enjoying it and the peaceful quiet. His hard body beneath T-shirt and jeans was as brown as his face. He was thoroughly happy with his well-earned vacation after the grueling races at Hialeah Park in Miami. There was no one around to tell him what to do. The Black was his sole responsibility. It was almost as it had been in the beginning, so long ago.

He watched a great heron in long-legged flight against the blue sky and listened to its raucous cry. He followed it as it flew low over a grove of tall coconut palms, the fronds moving languidly in the soft breeze.

His gaze returned to his horse and he found the

Black still lying on his back, his hind legs drawn up and forelegs spread outward. Alec smiled; it was a most unusual position for a horse who led such an active life. Perhaps the Black, too, was succumbing to the languor of this land.

Alec shifted his body in order to get into a more comfortable position on the fence. He wondered if this might not be an ideal place to raise horses. Henry Dailey had suggested as much before leaving to oversee the training of several two-year-olds in New York. Henry, his old friend and trainer, had suggested they might even purchase a small farm in this area as an annex to Hopeful Farm up north. They would move their young stock here and, perhaps, some of the older horses that needed a long rest in the sun.

It was not a new idea, Alec had reminded Henry, for the Ocala area in upper-central Florida had become very popular with horse breeders as a year-round operation.

"Too popular," Henry had answered. "Land is more costly there, and we don't need to be with the others. This area is worth considering. Think about it while I'm gone."

There were advantages and disadvantages to it, Alec thought. The area was more suitable for the growing of sugar cane and vegetables than pasture grass. It was reclaimed swampland, the soil a black carpet of peat muck. Beneath it, of course, was the solid bedrock of coral limestone that shaped and held the Florida peninsula.

The rich farmland had been reclaimed by a flood control basin which the United States Army Engineers

had constructed to contain the waters of Lake Okee-
chobee to the north. They had diverted the waters
which normally had flowed over this area and drifted
south to nourish the Everglades. It had meant thou-
sands of square miles of new agricultural land and com-
munities. But it also meant, Alec reflected bitterly, the
ultimate death of the great swamp. More and more
canals were being built, not only by the Army engineers but by private developers promising "residential
neighborhoods where wild animals once lived."

Alec turned and faced south, where he could see
an endless tawny blaze of light that seemed to merge
and mingle with the rays of the rising sun. He was at
the doorstep of the wild Everglades, and after what he
had read and heard of the immensity of the swamp, he
wondered if bulldozers and draglines would ever be
able to transform it completely into the realtors' promised Garden of Eden. He stared in that direction a long
time.

Finally, he roused himself, shaking his head and
wondering why on this morning he should be drawn to
the swamp, as if by a magnet, when he never had
thought much about it before.

Perhaps, he decided, the peace, the languor, or
whatever one wished to call it was changing his metab-
olism as it seemed to be doing to the Black this very
moment.

He jumped down from the fence, determined to
disturb the quiet of the morning. He rode the Black
daily, and today must be no exception. The spring racing season would open soon in New York and they
were scheduled to be there. Henry had given them a

few weeks to freshen up from their hard winter campaign but no more than that.

He walked over to his horse, wondering if he'd be able to acquire another paddock for him. It was the first time he'd seen mares turned out in the adjacent field, and he did not want the Black distracted. It was difficult enough in the spring of the year without having a band of broodmares in the next field! He knew that mares generally coped with the breeding season better than stallions; they possessed patience, whereas stallions, once started on a breeding program, felt only the persistent drive to mate.

He was glad Henry had not been around to see the mares in the adjacent pasture. He'd have raised the devil. It was an oversight, Alec knew, and he'd be able to straighten it out with Joe Early, the ranch manager, later in the day.

The Black had rolled over on his side and was the picture of a horse completely at ease. His eyes were open, and when he saw Alec coming toward him with the lead shank, he scrambled to his feet. He did not run away but stood still—as quiet as the morning—proud and long-limbed, waiting.

Alec snapped the shank on the halter ring. He never got tired of looking at his horse. He would always stand in awe of the Black, no matter how long he had him.

Few ever saw the true greatness in the Black without standing close to him. No picture could convey it. Nor could it be seen from fence rail or grandstand, as electric as his presence and speed might be. One had to stand beside him to appreciate the arrogance and nobility that were stamped on his small fine head. One had to rub him with soft cloths and brushes to see how well every part of his seventeen-hand body fitted together to make him the greatest runner of all time.

Alec watched the stallion's ears, for his horse talked with his ears. Now they flicked south in the direction of the Everglades.

Alec answered with his hands, running them down the arched neck. Then he said aloud, "You too? Okay, we'll go that way this morning if only for a change of scenery."

His fingers rubbed the ridge of the stallion's neck. "We're on vacation, you and I," he said. "We can do pretty much as we please with Henry gone."

There was a long sun-filled day ahead of them. Early up and early to bed, that alone was the rule on vacation and an easy one to keep.

"You're a good fellow," Alec said softly. The Black turned his head toward him, as if listening attentively. Alec knew that his horse understood the warmth of his words if not the precise meaning, and that was all that mattered. He felt the stallion's breath against his face. There was a gentleness, too, about his horse which few people ever saw. The large eyes gazed calmly and trustfully into his own.

"We'd probably get pretty lazy staying here all the time," he said. "You and I need a change of seasons. I don't think this place would be good for us at all."

The Black snorted.

"Not that we can't have fun here," Alec continued,

rubbing the soft muzzle. "And there's no reason why we can't see some of the swamp today. No reason at all."

He paused before mounting, aware of an odd feeling coming over him. It was vague but there, an awareness that this morning somehow was not like other mornings. He shrugged his shoulders. Today was like any other day, he told himself, except that he would ride south for a change and do some exploring.

He passed a hand along the stallion's backbone, waiting for the headiness, almost a feeling of momentary intoxication, to leave him. He decided that the feeling might be one of pure joy at having his horse to himself for a change.

It had taken three days of Henry's absence for him to realize how glad he was to be free of the trainer's yoke. He longed for complete abandon and freedom of movement, if only for a short while. Ahead of him was a long summer of racing, unremitting in its toil and preparation. And, when he wasn't racing, there was work to be done at Hopeful Farm. Good help was hard to get and even more difficult to keep. Every free day would be used to help repair fences and barns, to harrow paddocks, to care for the new foals and to cut, bale and store hay for the winter. One never caught up. Time taken out—even for racing—was never regained.

Alec thought longingly of the days when his every move did not have to be obedient and useful, when he could be off on the Black, to go where he liked and as he pleased.

"Why not ride bareback this morning?" he asked

DON'T FORGET THE STORY
THAT BEGAN IT ALL . . .

Alec Ramsay first saw the Black Stallion when his ship docked at a small Arabian port on the Red Sea. Little did he dream then that the magnificent wild horse was destined to play an important part in his young life; that the strange understanding which grew between them would lead through untold dangers to high adventure in America.

THE SECOND GREAT ADVENTURE
ABOUT ALEC AND THE BLACK

What was the motive of the night prowler in attempting to destroy the Black, one of the world's most famous horses? The prowler left behind him a gold medallion on which was embossed the figure of a large white bird, its wings outstretched in flight. Was it the Phoenix, the fabulous bird of mythology that symbolizes the resurrection of the dead?

THE THIRD BOOK IN THE CLASSIC BLACK STALLION SERIES

SON OF THE BLACK STALLION

When the Black Stallion's son arrives from Arabia, young Alec Ramsay believes his dreams have come true. Satan is everything a horse should be: beautiful, spirited, and intelligent. But veteran trainer Henry sees something dark and disturbing in the colt's stony gaze.